TWO *of a* KIND

JOSEPH CLARO

Photographs by Richard Hutchings

Copyright © 1989 by Scholastic Inc.
All rights reserved. Published by Scholastic Inc.
SPRINT and SPRINT BOOKS are trademarks of Scholastic Inc.
Printed in the U.S.A.
ISBN 0-590-35215-6

3 4 5 6 7 8 9 10   31   03 02 01 00 99 98 97

CHAPTER 1

"Did you see the new ninth-graders?" Tommy asked. He was sitting on the living room floor in front of the TV. "Were we that puny a year ago?"

"Yes, we were," Luke said. He was thumbing through a news magazine, looking for the science section. Then he looked up and added, "In fact, one of us still is." He stared straight at Tommy for a second to show which one he meant.

Tommy ignored the look. "Yeah, it's too bad you're such a runt, Luke," he said. "But cheer up — you still have me for a friend." He turned the TV on and flipped the channel selector until he found a music video. He left it on with the sound low.

"Here it is," Luke said, folding the news magazine open. "This is the article I want you to read."

"What's it about?" Tommy asked.

"Computer memory," Luke said. "They're making personal computers now with memories that can hold about a thousand times more information than ours can. I'm not sure how they work. But they're going to make home computers a whole different ball game."

"I'll read it later," Tommy said. "Then I'll explain it all to you."

"Maybe," Luke said with a grin. He tossed the

magazine to Tommy. "I'll ask Ms. Dolan about it tomorrow in science class. Just in case some of it is over your head."

They both looked at the video on the TV. Tommy tapped his foot to the beat of the music. Luke hummed along with the melody. Then he got up and stretched.

"Why don't we bring the baseball league up to date?" Luke asked.

"Good idea," Tommy said. Together, they ran upstairs to Tommy's room.

There were a lot of reasons why Luke and Tommy were good friends. One of the strongest reasons was their private baseball league. They had come up with the idea a year earlier.

They had named themselves the owners of two make-believe professional baseball teams. Each of them had selected twenty-five major-league players. These players covered all the positions of a real team. Once or twice a week, Luke and Tommy would check the newspapers to see how well their players had done. They would record every hit, every strikeout, and every error for each player.

Then they would use all this information to decide how many games each make-believe team had won. To do this, they used a complicated math formula. Luke had worked out the formula, with some help from Mr. Buxton, a math teacher at their school.

Tommy and Luke spent about an hour entering batting and pitching results in their league notebooks. Then they started looking through Tommy's collection of baseball cards.

"I had an idea about our league the other day," Tommy said.

"What was it?" Luke asked.

"We could turn it into a real league," Tommy said. "We could have eight or ten teams."

"It would take us days to record all the information," Luke said. "We wouldn't have time for anything but baseball statistics."

"No," Tommy said. "I didn't mean we should do it all ourselves. We could get other kids to form teams with us."

"That's a great idea!" Luke said. "Then we could have team standings, just like the real leagues. Maybe we could even play a world series at the end of the season."

"That's right," Tommy said. "I hadn't thought of that."

"Let's talk to some people at school tomorrow," Luke said. "I know Liz would want a team. And Manuel, and Kurt."

"You're right," Tommy said. "We'll ask them at school."

"Speaking of school," Luke said, "did you hear what Ms. Dolan said about tomorrow?"

"You mean about the 'exciting announcement' she's going to make?"

"Yeah. What do you think it could be?"

"Who knows?" Tommy said. "I hope it isn't something really boring, like a new math club or something."

"I doubt it," Luke said. "If Ms. Dolan says it's exciting, I think it will be exciting."

"We'll find out tomorrow, won't we?" Tommy said.

CHAPTER 2

The next morning a chilly rain put everyone in a bad mood. As people came into school, they shook off their coats and grumbled about the weather.

Luke rushed in through the main entrance. He stood in the middle of the entrance hall and shook his whole body.

"It's too early in the fall for this kind of weather!" he protested loudly.

Gina came into the entrance just in time to hear Luke's cry. "Don't let it get to you, Luke," she said. "By the time we leave today, it will probably be warm enough for swimming."

"Yeah," Luke said. "But what do I do about this lunch?"

He held up a damp brown paper bag. Just then Tommy and Liz came around a corner from the locker area.

"Is that bag up for auction?" Liz asked.

Luke grinned at her. Then he called out, "What am I bid, ladies and gentlemen? Here's your chance to own the world's soggiest peanut-butter-and-jelly sandwich. Can we start the bidding at one dollar?"

"One dollar it is!" a voice answered. A small circle began to form around Luke. He looked around to see who had made the offer.

"Deborah?" he said. "Was that you?"

"Yes," Deborah said. "Just give me the dollar,

and I'll take that sad-looking bag off your hands."

Several people groaned at the awful joke. Luke let his body slump. He dropped the bag onto the floor and grinned at Tommy and Liz. They were both laughing.

"Hey, Luke," Liz said. "I see you can clown around even on a miserable day."

Luke bent down to pick up his lunch bag. "Yeah. Well," he said, "you guys are always so grouchy on a day like this, I feel it's my duty to cheer you up."

Two hours later, everyone was feeling a little better. The rain had stopped. The sun was shining. And it was getting warmer by the minute.

Luke and Tommy met outside Ms. Dolan's room. This was the first class of the day they had together.

"How was English?" Tommy asked.

"Not bad," Luke said. "We're reading *Huckleberry Finn*. Mr. Garoli loves to ham it up reading that stuff aloud. Actually, he's a lot of fun to listen to."

"I heard he used to be an actor," Tommy said.

They walked into the classroom and took seats at the same table. Ms. Dolan came in a few seconds later. She began taking attendance.

Gina called out from the back of the room. "Ms. Dolan," she said. "What about that announcement you mentioned yesterday?"

"I haven't forgotten it, Gina," Ms. Dolan answered. "I'll get to it. Just let me go over the new lab assignments."

That made everyone a little fidgety. Ms. Dolan had ended yesterday's class with a hint of some mysterious announcement. Now they were going to have to wait just a little longer to find out what it was.

Going over the lab assignments always took time. First, Ms. Dolan would give everyone an assigned topic. Then she would go over the

available lab hours. Some people had to be given new assignments because of time conflicts. Then the new assignments might affect somebody else's schedule. All in all, it took thirty minutes to get the whole thing done.

When it was over, Ms. Dolan said, "All right. Now, let's talk about that announcement."

All heads turned to the front. Several people sat up a little straighter. Everyone was paying attention.

"The announcement concerns two important subjects," Ms. Dolan said, smiling. "Science and

money. Three organizations in town have put together a contest. There's one for each grade level in high school. The sophomore contest carries a first prize of $2,000."

Ms. Dolan sat down in her chair. She looked as if she expected a boisterous reaction, and that was what she got. There were cheers and whistles. There were cries of "Two thousand dollars!" People exchanged grins. They slapped one another on the back and laughed loudly. Ms. Dolan sat quietly. She was waiting for the noise to die down.

"Ms. Dolan," George called over the noise. "What do we have to do to win the money?"

"I'd be happy to tell you," she said. "As soon as everyone calms down, I will."

"Shhh! Quiet down!" George said. He was soon joined by others. They all wanted to hear the rest of the announcement. When it was quiet, Miss Dolan stood up again.

"The contest is a simple one," she said. "But that doesn't mean it will be easy to win. You have to design or build something that will do one of two things. Either it has to improve the lives of a large number of people, or it has to provide entertainment. Your product must be original. But it can be based on something that exists now."

"How much time do we have to do this?" Luke asked.

"The projects are due January 15," Ms. Dolan said. "That means you have three and a half months to work on them."

"How can we be sure we have an original idea?" Laura asked. "I mean, suppose I make something, and it already exists."

"Your project won't be considered unless your science teacher has approved it," Ms. Dolan said. "And I won't approve it unless the judges agree that it's original."

"Do we have to work alone?" Tommy asked.

"Certainly not," Ms. Dolan said. Tommy and

Luke exchanged glances and smiled at each other. "In fact," she went on, "I'd suggest you all consider working with a partner. It means splitting the prize money, of course. But half of $2,000 is better than a hundred percent of nothing."

Most of the people in the class seemed to agree with this idea. Within seconds, people were matching up with their friends. There was a lot of excitement about the projects. There was even more about the money.

"Two thousand dollars," George said. "Think about it. I could buy a car the day after I got my license."

"I'm afraid not," Ms. Dolan said. "Everyone listen up, please." The class quieted down again.

"You won't get the money right away," she said. "The contest is meant to encourage you to go to college. So the money won't be available until you finish high school."

There were a few groans from the back of the room.

Ms. Dolan looked at George. "At that point," she said, "you still might want to spend it on a car. Or you might want to use it for college. But you won't be able to decide until then."

The bell rang, as though Ms. Dolan had timed it. Everyone gathered up books and lunch bags and moved toward the door. Luke and Tommy walked out together.

"Got any ideas?" Luke asked.

"One or two," Tommy said. "How about you?"

"A couple," Luke said. "When can we talk?"

"Well, I won't be at lunch today," Tommy said.
"I have to do some work in the library. Let's talk
about it on the way home."

"Okay," Luke said. "See you at three o'clock."

CHAPTER 3

Luke and Tommy met at the bicycle rack after school. The bikes were dry, but the wheels were covered with mud from the morning rain. They spent a couple of minutes scraping the mud off the tires. Then they hopped on their bikes and began slowly pedaling home.

"What do you think our project should be?" Luke asked.

"I've got one idea that I think would be pretty interesting," Tommy answered. "The only trouble is, it involves work in chemistry."

"What is it?" Luke asked.

"Well, I thought we might be able to come up with something that *really* makes children's aspirin taste better. We could find out what they use now. You know, that stuff that tastes like a Martian's idea of orange candy. And we could try to improve on it."

"That would be great," Luke said. "But do we know enough about chemistry to do that?"

"Probably not," Tommy admitted.

"I thought maybe we could build a trash compactor," Luke said. "But then I realized it would call for expensive equipment."

"It wouldn't *have* to be expensive, would it?" asked Tommy.

"I'm afraid it would. I was thinking of a big one — a compactor that would service a whole neighborhood," Luke said.

They decided to stop at the playground and use the basketball court. Luke believed that shooting baskets relaxed his mind. He went into the attendant's office to get a ball. Tommy locked both their bikes to the rack.

Luke came out, dribbling a basketball. "So chemistry is out," he said. He tossed the ball toward the basket. It hit the backboard, circled the rim, and fell through.

"Lucky shot," Tommy said.

"Nope," Luke said. "I planned it just that way."

Tommy picked up the ball. He began dribbling it low to the ground. He faked left and right, even though Luke wasn't guarding him. Then he suddenly spun around. He raised his right arm into the air. He pushed the ball toward the basket. It fell right through the hoop.

"*That's* the way to shoot a basket," he said. "And chemistry isn't the only thing that's out."

"What do you mean?" Luke asked. He grabbed the ball and shot another basket.

"We can't do anything that involves too much physics."

"Why not?"

"I don't like to have to remind you of this," Tommy said. "But we don't know anything about physics."

"Yeah, that is a drawback," Luke said, tossing the ball.

"What we should do," Tommy said, "is stick

with something we really know about."

Luke looked at his watch. "We'd better get going," he said. "I have to get dinner started before I do my homework."

He returned the ball to the attendant. Tommy unlocked the bikes, and they started home.

"All right," Tommy said. "What do we really know about?"

"How about earth science?" Luke said.

"How about it?" Tommy asked. "Maybe we could invent a new kind of rain."

Luke ignored the weak attempt at a joke. "There's only one thing left," he said. "Computers."

They both fell silent. This was definitely the area they would work in. Neither of them was a computer genius. But they both enjoyed working with computers as much as anything else they did together.

By the time they reached Luke's house, they had a few good ideas to play with. And the more they talked about them, the more excited they became.

"I can't stay," Tommy said. "But let's see what we have so far. It has to have something to do with personal computers."

"Right," Luke said. "That way, we can be sure a lot of people will be able to use it. And it has to be either helpful or entertaining."

"And it can't cost too much," Tommy added.

"Okay," Luke said. "That's a start. Let's think about it and see what we come up with. Maybe we can talk about it tonight."

Tommy nodded. "Talk to you later," he said. He rode home deep in thought.

Luke came to Tommy's house after dinner. They both went immediately up to Tommy's room. About an hour later, they came charging down the stairs.

"Easy, boys!" Tommy's mother called out. She was working at her desk in the living room. Her husband was sitting on the couch, reading a magazine.

"Mr. and Mrs. Andersen!" Luke said. "We have something worked out, and we want to know what you think."

"Something worked out?" Mr. Andersen said.

"For the science project," Tommy said. "I told you about it at dinner."

"Oh, yes," Mr. Andersen said. "I didn't think you'd come up with something so soon."

Mrs. Andersen put her papers away. She sat on the couch next to her husband. "Tell us about it," she said.

Tommy looked at Luke. "Go ahead," Luke said. "It's your living room."

"All right," Tommy said, standing in front of the couch. "We want to write a computer program. It would be a baseball league."

"You mean to keep track of how different players perform in a season?" Mrs. Andersen asked.

"Sort of," Luke said. "I mean, it would keep track of a player's statistics. But not for the league he really plays in."

"I don't understand," Mr. Andersen said. "What other league would be interested in a player's statistics?"

"Our league," Tommy answered. "The league that Luke and I invented last year."

"Oh, I get it," Mrs. Andersen said. "You're thinking of all that time the two of you spend entering figures in your notebooks."

"And your program would make all that easier to do," Mr. Andersen said.

"Right," Luke said. "But that's only part of it. Right now, we have only two teams. We've been thinking about expanding the league. With this new program, that would be really easy to do."

"Sounds great," Mr. Andersen said. "Can you two really write a program like this?"

"We think we can," Tommy said.

"We could write a program for one team in just a few days," Luke said. "The real problem is writing one that will work for eight or ten teams."

"Or more," Tommy added.

Mr. Andersen grinned. "I'm really impressed," he said. "You guys make me ashamed of how I spent my own teenage years."

"How did you spend them, Dad?" Tommy asked, smiling.

"Never mind," Mr. Andersen said. "I congratulate both of you on even getting this far. You have a great idea."

"If there's any way we can help," Mrs. Andersen said, "let us know. Although I can't imagine what we might do."

"Thanks," Luke said. "We just wanted to check with you. We wanted to make sure it wasn't a crazy idea."

"Anything but crazy," Mr. Andersen said. "Go to it."

CHAPTER 4

"Tommy," Liz called. "Tommy, wait!"

Tommy was walking home from school. He turned and saw Liz trotting to catch up to him.

"Hi," he said, as she reached him.

"Hi. Where's your bike?"

"I had to leave it home. The front tire was flat, and I was already a little late. So I didn't have time to change it. How have you been?"

"Pretty good," Liz said. "You certainly have been hard to find these past two weeks."

"Yeah. Once Luke and I got started on that project, we stopped doing everything else."

"Where is Luke?" she asked. "I don't think I saw him today."

"No," Tommy said. "He didn't come to school. He called me last night. He said he was staying home. Sounded terrible. I guess it's a cold or something."

"So," Liz said, "what about your project? I heard Ms. Dolan was raving about it in one of her classes yesterday."

"Really?" Tommy said, pleased. "Luke will be glad to hear that."

"I only heard about it in bits and pieces," Liz said. "Tell me what you guys are cooking up."

"It's still mostly on paper," Tommy said. "But we've actually managed to get some parts of the program to work. It's for a make-believe baseball league that uses real players."

"You mean real major-league players?" Liz asked.

"Right. At the beginning of a season, we'll get about ten people together. Each of them will become the owner of a team. We'll all pick players for our teams. That's where the computer program will take over."

"What will it do?" Liz asked.

"First, it will ask for information about what each player did during a week. We'll take turns entering this information."

"So far," Liz said, "you've done more work than the computer has."

"Right," Tommy said. "But after that, the computer does all the work. It looks at what each player on a team has done. Then it decides how many games the team has won and lost that week. So we'll have standings, just like the real major leagues. At the end of the season, we'll have a pennant winner."

"That sounds terrific," Liz said. "Suppose you ran a league like this without a computer. How much work would you have to do?"

"Luke was wondering about that same question last week," Tommy said. "He figured out what the computer would be doing. Then he figured out how much time it would take the two of us."

"What did he come up with?" Liz asked.

"It would take us seven days a week to do it," Tommy said. "But only if there were about 30 hours in a day."

Liz laughed. "In other words," she said, "it would be impossible."

"Right."

"In that case," she said, "you've probably invented a fantastic program."

"Well," Tommy said, "we don't have it yet. We still have a long way to go."

"But you have it all worked out in your heads?"

"Yep," Tommy said. "But a lot of work goes into getting the computer to do what we want it to do."

"I don't have any doubt that you two will pull it off," Liz said.

"Thanks," Tommy said.

They reached the corner where Liz had to turn off. "Tell Luke I hope he feels better," she called over her shoulder as she walked away.

"Okay, I'll tell him," Tommy said. "See you tomorrow."

Tommy went inside his house, poured himself a glass of orange juice, and sprawled on the couch. He took a few sips of the juice. Then he put the glass down and dialed Luke's number. It rang seven or eight times, with no answer.

That was strange, Tommy thought. Luke said he'd be staying home all day. Maybe he had dialed a wrong number. He hung up and tried again. This time it rang five times before someone answered.

"Hello?" Luke said.

"Luke?"

"Yeah."

"This is Tommy."

"I know. How's it going?"

"Okay. How's your cold?"

"My what?" Luke said. He didn't seem to be paying much attention.

"Your cold," Tommy repeated.

"Oh. Much better, thanks."

"Listen," Tommy said. "Did your phone just ring seven or eight times, about a minute ago?"

"My phone?" Luke asked. "No, uh, I don't think so. Why?"

He sounded strange to Tommy. He sounded as though he didn't even want to be talking.

"Never mind," Tommy said. "It isn't important. Aren't you going to ask me why I called?"

"Huh?" Luke said. "Yeah. Sure."

Tommy paused. "Luke," he asked, "is anything wrong?"

"Wrong? No. Why did you call?"

"I wanted to ask you about the program. Did you talk to your uncle?"

"About what?" Luke said.

Now Tommy was getting annoyed. "About the problem we're having. You know, when the computer sometimes puts the figures into the wrong team. Remember? Your uncle, who's a computer programmer?"

"Oh, yeah," Luke said. "I'm sorry. Of course I remember. But no, I didn't ask him. I figured I'd call him over the weekend."

Tommy was having trouble believing this was really Luke on the other end of the phone. But he knew his friend's voice.

"Luke," he said, "are you sure nothing is wrong?"

"I said nothing is wrong!" Luke snapped back. "What would be wrong? Look, don't worry about the program, will you? I said I'd ask my uncle. And I will ask him. But it can wait till Saturday, can't it?"

"Sure," Tommy said softly. "Sure, it can wait."

"Okay."

"I'd better be going," Tommy said. "Will you be in school tomorrow?"

"Yes," Luke said. "Well, maybe."

"Okay," Tommy said. "See you then."

"Right. So long."

Tommy heard the click on the other end of the phone. Then he hung up himself. *Now what was that all about?* he thought. *He sounded like a stranger.*

No matter what Luke had said, Tommy knew that something was wrong. Something was bothering Luke. And it was something he wouldn't tell even his best friend about.

Shaking his head in confusion, Tommy went upstairs to do his homework.

CHAPTER 5

The next day was Friday. Luke didn't show up at school. Tommy spent most of the day trying to decide whether or not to call him. He couldn't make any sense of the conversation they'd had on Thursday afternoon. He finally decided not to call.

Right after breakfast on Saturday morning, Tommy rode his bike to Luke's house. The car wasn't parked in front of the house. Tommy couldn't tell whether or not anyone was home.

He rang the bell and waited. After about a minute, he rang it again. Then he heard footsteps from inside. The door opened, and Luke stood in the doorway. He looked tired, or sick, Tommy thought.

"Hey," Tommy said, forcing a smile. "How's it going?"

"Okay," Luke said. "How about you?"

"Pretty good. Can I come in?"

Luke hesitated for a few seconds. Then he said, "Sure. Sure, come on in."

He stepped aside to let Tommy in. Then he closed the door. Both boys went into the living room. Tommy sat on the couch. Luke stood near the window.

"You here alone?" Tommy asked.

"Yeah," Luke said. "My parents . . . had to go someplace."

Tommy had a dozen questions bouncing around in his head. *Have you been sick?* he wanted to ask. *Are you mad at me? Is something wrong?*

But he wouldn't ask any of the questions. He kept remembering Thursday's phone call. He didn't want to trigger another reaction like that. Instead, he decided to stick to their project.

"We have a lot of work to do on the program," he said.

"Yeah," Luke said, not looking at him. "I guess we have."

"I thought we should set up some kind of schedule," Tommy said. "You know, divide the work and agree on deadlines."

"Divide the work?" Luke said. "How are we going to do that? I thought we were supposed to do it all together."

"Well, yeah," Tommy said. "That was our original plan. But I thought you might want to talk about changing the plan."

"Why?" Luke asked. Tommy thought he sounded strange — sort of suspicious.

"I don't know," Tommy said. "Things don't seem to be working very smoothly with the current plan."

"You're talking about my uncle again, aren't you?" Luke said.

"No, I — "

"Look, I said I'd call him. And I will." Now he sounded definitely angry. "You want me to apologize for holding up the schedule? Okay, I'm sorry."

"I wasn't thinking about that," Tommy said. "I just mean in general . . ."

"In general, what?" Luke said.

"Well, we haven't been making much progress," Tommy said. "This has been a pretty slow week. You have to admit that, don't you?"

"Yeah," Luke said, throwing himself into an easy chair. "I guess I do have to admit that. It isn't working out the way we thought it would."

"I've tried to keep things on schedule," Tommy said. "But it's a two-man operation."

"And only one man has been doing the work," Luke said. "All right, I get the message."

"I didn't come here to give you a message," Tommy said.

"What did you come for?"

Tommy was stunned by the question. Did Luke really want an answer? Was this the same Luke that Tommy had been such close friends with for years? What was going on here?

"Listen," Tommy said, "maybe you want to think things over by yourself."

"Think what over?" Luke said. He was angry again. "You want me to reconsider the project? What do I have to think over? Whether I'm good enough to work with somebody who carries my weight for me?"

"Come on, Luke," Tommy said. "I don't want to fight with you. I just — "

"Maybe I'm not good enough," Luke said, standing over Tommy. "Maybe you can do the project better on your own."

"Who said anything about — "

"In fact, that sounds like a good idea," Luke said. He turned and walked over to the window. He talked with his back to Tommy. "I don't know about you. But *I* sure could do a better job on my own."

"Luke!" Tommy said. "I don't want to do it alone."

Luke turned to face him. "Well, I don't want to listen to your complaining anymore," he said. "So you're going to have to do it alone. You can have it all. The whole idea now belongs to you. I have an idea for a better project. Only this one will get me the whole prize, not just a share."

He turned to look out the window again.

Tommy waited for a long time before speaking. Then he said, "Luke, this is crazy. I don't even know how we got into this argument.

I just came over to see how you were doing."

"I'm doing fine," Luke said. "I'll be doing even better after you've left."

"Okay," Tommy said. "I don't know what's going on. Something's bothering you — "

"*Nothing's bothering me!*" Luke said. He had turned around to face Tommy, and his teeth were clenched.

The two boys stood staring at each other for a long time. Luke was the first to look away.

Tommy took a deep breath. He decided it would be better not to say anything more. He turned and walked out of the room. He pulled the front door shut behind him. Then he got on his bike and slowly rode home.

CHAPTER 6

Tommy sat on his couch, staring at the TV. He was looking at a cartoon show. He had the sound turned low. He could just barely hear sound effects and some frantic kind of music. But if anyone had asked him what show it was, he wouldn't have been able to answer.

Tommy's father came into the room. "Saturday morning cartoons?" he said. "You haven't watched Saturday morning television in years."

Tommy looked up at him. "I'm not exactly watching," he said. "Just sort of . . . looking."

His father gave him a long, hard look. "I see," he said. He sat on the end of the couch opposite his son. "What's up?" he asked.

Tommy used the remote control to turn the sound all the way down. "Something really weird is going on," he said. "With Luke."

"Did you two have an argument?"

"Yes," Tommy said. "Well, no, not really. I mean, Luke had an argument. But I didn't."

"What do you mean?" his father asked.

"I'm not sure," Tommy said. "Luke seems to be mad at me. But I didn't do anything to make him mad."

"Exactly what happened?"

Tommy told his father about the phone conversation on Thursday. Then he told him what had happened earlier that morning. Mr. Andersen listened without saying anything.

"And he told me he wanted me to leave," Tommy said. "Luke practically threw me out of his house! After all I've done for him!"

"Take it easy," Mr. Andersen said. "Try not to say anything foolish. You've never done anything for Luke."

"How about — "

"Everything you've done has been because he's your friend," his father said. "When you do something for a friend, it isn't a favor. It's just a way of showing your affection."

Tommy sat in silence for a while, staring at the TV. Finally, he said, "You're right, Dad."

"I'm always right," his father said, smiling. "That's why I get to be the father."

"But what could be going on in his head?" Tommy asked. "I haven't done anything to make him mad, Dad. I really haven't."

"I believe you," his father said. "But you can't always know everything about a person, even when that person is your best friend. Who knows what might have set off Luke's anger? Maybe you said something that he took the wrong way."

"You think so?" Tommy asked.

"Could be. Or maybe he's having trouble with the computer project. Anger could be a way of hiding the trouble from himself. Or the problem could have nothing to do with you at all."

"What do you mean?" Tommy asked.

"Do you remember that argument your mother and I had last month? When we were yelling about who should be responsible for seeing that the gas tank is full?"

Tommy nodded.

"Well, the gas tank had nothing to do with the real problem. That whole dumb argument came about because your mother was having some trouble at work. We were arguing over something that wasn't really a problem between the two of us. It took us two days to figure that out."

"But what does this have to do with me and Luke?"

"Luke might have something on his mind. He might be upset over something you know nothing about. You have to try not to take his remarks personally. They just might have nothing to do with you."

They talked for a few more minutes. Then Tommy said he was going to talk with Liz.

"Thanks, Dad," he said, as he went out the door. "I feel a little better about things right now."

As he pedaled his bike to Liz's house, Tommy realized that he didn't really feel better. He was still annoyed with Luke. Maybe his father was right. Maybe Luke had something on his mind. But why couldn't he tell his best friend? Wasn't that what it meant to be best friends? Didn't it mean that you told each other everything?

Liz had barely opened the door when Tommy began to blurt out everything that had happened. He told her about the phone conversation and about his visit to Luke's house. He might have exaggerated a little when he told her how angry Luke had been, but, mostly, he told her exactly what had gone on.

"Is all this true?" Liz asked. "I mean, it doesn't sound like Luke at all."

"Nevertheless, it's all true," Tommy said. "Every word of it."

"What are you going to do?" she asked.

"Well," Tommy said, "he was crystal clear about one thing. He doesn't want to keep working on the project with me. So the first thing I have to do is find a new partner."

"How will you do that?" Liz asked. "Everybody else is already working on a project."

"You aren't," he said.

"No, but that's because I'm waiting for the math contest in February. I've always been more comfortable with math than with science projects. You know that."

"But February is months away," Tommy said. "And I need help now."

"Maybe you do," Liz said. "And maybe you don't. A lot of people would say that you could easily do this project on your own. In fact, I'd be one of those people."

"But I don't want to work alone," he said.

"I know that," Liz said. "But I think you're moving too fast. I mean, until three days ago, you and Luke were a team."

"That's all over now," Tommy said.

"I'm not sure," Liz said. "I find it hard to believe that Luke could suddenly break off a friendship that has lasted for so long."

"But you didn't see him this morning," Tommy replied. "And you didn't hear the anger in his voice."

"I know," she said. "But I still don't believe he

meant it. I'd bet a million dollars that he'll ask
you to forget everything he said."

Tommy looked up at her out of the corner of
his eye. "I'd take that bet," he said. "But I just
spent my last million."

"You think the same thing, don't you?" Liz
said. "You think he's going to come to his
senses."

"I hope he does," Tommy said. "But after being thrown out of his house, I'm not sure what I think. Are you sure you won't reconsider?"

"I'm positive," Liz said. "That project belongs to you and Luke. Just be patient."

Tommy sighed and rolled his eyes toward the ceiling. *It's easy to give advice,* he thought, *when you're not feeling the pain.*

CHAPTER 7

Monday was a tough day for Tommy. Luke was in school, but he made a point of avoiding Tommy. In fact, he seemed to be avoiding everybody. This puzzled a lot of people, because Luke was known as one of the friendliest people in school.

During the day, six or seven people asked Tommy whether something was wrong with his friend. Tommy kept mumbling about Luke having something on his mind. Then he'd hurry away, so he wouldn't have to say any more than that.

When he got home from school, he found a note his mother had taped to the refrigerator. She needed a few things from the supermarket for dinner. Tommy decided he'd better take care of that right away, before he got started on his homework.

He rode his bike to the supermarket. Inside, he raced up and down the aisles. He picked out the four items his mother wanted. Then he got on the express checkout line.

There were a lot of baskets in the express line. Tommy counted nine baskets in front of his. There was nothing to do now but wait.

He was aware of a dozen conversations going on around him. He wasn't listening to any of them, but they were seeping into his mind anyway. Then he realized that he *had* been half-listening to one conversation. The two women in

front of him were talking about an electronics company. The company owned a big plant on the north side of town.

"They're closing down more than half of their operations," one woman said. "Over two hundred people will be out of work."

"It happens every few years," the other woman said. "There just seems to be no protection against it."

As the line moved forward, Tommy ran the conversation back in his head. Although he hadn't been paying attention, he had heard the name of the company. Reese Industries owned the plant the women were talking about.

Suddenly, he couldn't wait to get out of the supermarket. There were now only two people in front of him. But it seemed to take years for the checker to get through with them. When Tommy reached the front of the line, he packed his stuff himself. He quickly paid the clerk and rushed out of the supermarket.

Instead of going home, Tommy rode to the library. The librarian showed him where to find back issues of newspapers.

He pulled out the last three weeks' issues of the local newspaper. Then he started working backwards through the papers. He ran his eye over headlines, looking for local business news.

Then he found what he was looking for. Ten days before, the newspaper had carried an article about Reese Industries. The company had just finished a government contract, the article said. They had been counting on getting another one right away. But government spending was being cut back. That meant there would be no new contract. As a result, Reese was letting hundreds of people go. The aerospace department was hit harder than any other.

Tommy left the library and rode north. The Reese plant was about five miles from the library. Twenty minutes later, he pulled up at the gate outside the factory.

The guard stepped out of his booth at the gate. "Can I help you, son?" he asked.

"Uh, I'm looking for someone who works here," Tommy said.

"A lot of people work here," the guard said. "Do you know what department he works in?"

"Aerospace," Tommy said.

"That's not a department," the guard said. "That's a whole division of the company."

"How do I find him?" Tommy asked.

"I guess you could try personnel," the guard said. "It's in that building over there. I'll call and let them know you're coming."

"Thanks," Tommy said, beginning to pedal toward the building.

Inside, he found the personnel office with no trouble. A woman was sitting at a reception desk.

"Hello," she said pleasantly. "You must be the young man the guard just called me about."

"Yes," Tommy said. "My name is Tommy Andersen. I'm trying to get in touch with a friend. That is, he's my friend's father. He works

here. I want to get a message to him."

"What's your friend's name?"

"Snider," Tommy said. Then he had to think hard to remember Mr. Snider's first name. Was it Arthur? Andrew? "Arnold Snider," he said. "He works in the aerospace division."

"Just a minute," the woman said. She went to the back of the room and opened a large file drawer. Tommy watched her searching through the files for several minutes. Then she came back, holding a large folder.

"Arnold Snider," she said. "Do you happen to know his address?"

"Sure," Tommy said. "He lives at 1602 Marathon Drive."

"Yes," the woman said. "This is the one. I'm afraid I can't help you, though. Your friend isn't with us right now."

"Isn't with you?"

"No," the woman said. "We've recently lost a lot of work in aerospace. We've cut a lot of jobs in that division. Mr. Snider's job, I'm sorry to say, was one of them."

That was exactly what Tommy had expected to hear. Luke's father had lost his job. That must be what was behind Luke's strange behavior. That had to be it.

"Oh, I see," Tommy said. "Well, thank you."

He ran out to his bike and raced all the way home.

CHAPTER 8

When Tommy got home, it was nearly 5:00. He put the groceries away, then wrote a note to his parents.

> *Went to Luke's house. I may be there a while. If I'm late, have dinner without me. I'll eat later. I'm sorry if this annoys you, but it's really important. See you later.*

He rode over to Luke's house. He put his bike in the driveway near the garage. Then he rang the front doorbell.

"Oh! Hi, Mr. Snider," he said, when the door opened. "I . . . I just came over to see Luke. Is he home?"

He was having trouble looking Mr. Snider in the eye. He didn't like knowing a "family secret." It was a funny feeling.

"Yes, he's home," Mr. Snider said pleasantly. "Come on in, Tommy." He turned to the stairs and called, "Luke! Luke, Tommy's here."

Luke didn't answer. Mr. Snider said, "Go ahead up. Maybe he didn't hear me. He probably has his headset on."

Tommy went slowly upstairs. In his mind he kept seeing Luke's angry face telling him to leave. He reached Luke's room and knocked.

"Who is it?"

"It's me. Tommy."

"Come on in," Luke said.

Tommy hesitated for a moment and then walked into the room. Luke was sitting on his bed, holding his trumpet.

"I wanted to talk to you," Tommy said.

"Yeah," Luke said. "I have to talk to you, too."

"Are you making any progress working on your own?" Tommy asked.

Luke shook his head. "I haven't even thought about it," he said. "How are you coming along?"

"Not so good," Tommy said. "I haven't done much either."

"Look," Luke said, "I'm sorry about the other day. I was way out of line."

"Does that mean you've changed your mind?" Tommy asked.

"No," Luke said quickly. "I'm not going to work on the project with you. I just wanted you to know I didn't mean those things I said."

"I really want you to reconsider," Tommy said.

"I can't do it, Tommy," Luke said. "I'd be wasting your time. And I'd probably keep you from winning the prize."

"And you won't tell me why?" Tommy said.

"No. I don't know why. I mean, I don't have any reason, really. I've just lost interest in the whole thing."

"Does it have anything to do with your father?"

Luke looked at Tommy, surprised.

"I mean," Tommy went on, "with his losing his job and all."

Luke looked puzzled. He also looked angry.

"Who told you he lost his job?" he asked.

"Nobody," Tommy said. "I found out about it on my own."

Luke didn't say anything for a long time. Then he took a deep breath.

"It happened almost two weeks ago," he said. "Everything was going smoothly. Then my father came home with this news. He's worked at that company for eight years. All of a sudden, they just told him to go home."

"Can't he get another job?"

"He's been looking ever since he heard the bad news," Luke said. "When he isn't out on an interview, he's on the phone. The whole thing has made him miserable. Even my mother can't talk to him. They just argue all day long."

Luke looked down at his trumpet. Tommy waited a while before asking his next question.

"So," he said finally, "what will *you* do about all this?"

Luke looked up at Tommy. "What do you mean?" he asked. "What can I do?"

"About your father's problem?" Tommy said. "Probably nothing. But how about your problem?"

"What's my problem?"

"I'm not sure," Tommy said. "But you're acting as though your whole life has come to an end."

"Maybe I am," Luke mumbled. "But that's because there's one other thing I haven't told you."

"What's that?" Tommy asked.

Luke didn't say anything for a long time. Tommy was beginning to wonder if he'd heard the question. Finally, Luke let out a sigh. "There's one job he might possibly get," he said. "It's in Ashton."

"Ashton!" Tommy exclaimed in surprise. "But Ashton must be a couple of hundred miles from here!"

"Two hundred and sixty-three miles, to be exact. I looked it up," Luke said.

"Oh," Tommy said quietly. "So if he takes this job — "

"We'll have to move," Luke said.

They were quiet for a long time. Finally, Tommy broke the silence.

"So what?" he said.

Luke looked at him, puzzled. "What does 'so what' mean?" he asked.

"So what if you have to move?" Tommy said.

"So what?" Luke said. "So I'll have to leave this house. So I'll have to leave my friends. That's so what."

"It's only a couple of hundred miles," Tommy said.

"Two hundred and — "

"I know, I know," Tommy interrupted. "But it isn't as though you'd be moving to South America, you know."

"Might as well be," Luke said.

"Wrong," Tommy said. "In the first place, you can get from here to Ashton in about four hours. In the second place, there's this new invention. You know, you hook it up to your phone? Then you can type computer messages back and forth? Maybe you've heard of it. I think they call it a modem."

Luke was smiling. "The word does sound familiar," he said.

"Besides," Tommy said, "you don't even know if you'll have to move. That's the worst thing that could happen. But it hasn't happened yet."

"I guess not," Luke said.

There was another long pause. Then Luke said, "I guess I should have told you about my father."

"Maybe," Tommy said. "While I was riding over here, I kept thinking about that. On the one hand, you might say, 'What good is having a friend, if you can't go to him when things get bad?' But there's another side."

"What's that?" Luke asked.

"Maybe there are some things you have to keep to yourself," Tommy said. "Maybe you don't tell even your best friend some things."

"That's how I've felt the last two weeks," Luke said. "I didn't even want you to know about it. But now I'm glad you do."

"Good," Tommy said. "Just remember this: Anybody can be your friend when you have no problems. I'm the one you can count on when the ceiling falls in."

"I know," Luke said. "I guess I just forgot."

"Okay," Tommy said. "Let's take stock. Your parents are in a bad way right now. And that's making you miserable."

"You don't know how miserable," Luke said.

"Of course I don't, you dummy. You've refused to talk to me about it. Now, you can't get your father another job. And you can't keep him from taking a job in Ashton. But you can do one thing."

"What's that, O Wise One?"

"You can keep yourself from falling into a pit just because your parents are having trouble right now. And how do you do that?"

"Tell me," Luke said, grinning.

"You get back on track," Tommy said. "You make up for lost time on this project."

Luke was quiet for a moment. Then he smiled at Tommy. "You're absolutely right," he said. "I hope my father can find something. And I sure hope it's closer to home than Ashton. I also hope my parents stop fighting all the time. But I can't do anything about any of those problems."

"There's one other reason you have to get back on the project," Tommy said.

"What's that?"

"Well, I hate to admit it in your presence, but I can't do it alone."

Luke laughed. Then he looked at his watch. "Can you stay for dinner?" he asked.

"No," Tommy said. "I think my parents may already have the state police on my trail. I'd better be going."

Luke walked him to the front door. "See you tomorrow," he said.

"Can we get back to work tomorrow?" Tommy asked.

"Sure," Luke said. Tommy started out toward the driveway. "So long!" Luke called after him.

Tommy waved. Then he went around the side of the house to get his bike.

CHAPTER 9

After Tommy left, Luke went into the living room. His father was watching a baseball game on TV. Luke sat on the couch and looked at the game for a few minutes.

Mr. Snider got up and turned off the TV. "Do you want to talk about it?" he asked.

Luke looked up at him. After a few seconds, he said, "Yeah. I think I do."

Mr. Snider waited. When Luke didn't say anything, he spoke himself.

"I have a pretty good idea of what's been going on," he said. "Did you and Tommy have an argument?"

"Sort of," Luke said. "The other day, I told him I was dropping out of the science project. But he hadn't done anything to bring it on."

"So you had no reason to be angry with him?" Mr. Snider asked.

"No," Luke said. "It wasn't him I was angry with." He paused and looked hard at his father. "I guess it was you," he said. "You and Mom."

Mr. Snider nodded. "That isn't surprising," he said. "I guess we've been making things pretty uncomfortable around here for you lately. No — that isn't exactly right. *I've* been making things tough for both of you."

"Dad," Luke said, "I know this isn't your fault."

"Getting fired isn't my fault," Mr. Snider said.

"But taking it out on your mother is."

He paused for a moment and then went on. "Things like this happen to everybody," he said. "Life goes along nicely for a long time. Then suddenly the ground collapses under your feet. So, for a while, I've been scared. I've been wondering if I'll be able to put things back together again."

He stopped talking and stared out the window. Then he turned back to Luke.

"Well, I will get things back together somehow," he said. "But that's my problem, not yours. You didn't lose your job. I did. Except for the atmosphere around here, your life hasn't really changed at all. It would be crazy to throw away something as important as your science project. Whenever something like this happens, you have to shake off the punch and get right back to what you were doing."

Luke let out a sigh. He felt as though he'd just dropped an enormous backpack to the floor.

"One other thing," Mr. Snider said. "About Tommy. You have a valuable friend there. You want to be very careful how you treat him. Sure, you should tell him off if he steps out of line. But don't ever take out your problems on him. A real friend is worth too much to be abused. And I think you have a real friend there."

"I know I have," Luke said. "I treated him like dirt the other day. And you know what he did?

He asked around and found out what was really bothering me. And he came back to see if he could help."

"As I said, a real friend," Mr. Snider said.

He turned the TV back on. The two of them sat watching the game in silence for a few

minutes. Then Luke hopped to his feet.

"I'll be back before dinner," he said.

"Where are you going?"

Luke turned and faced his father. "I'm going to ride over and thank my friend," he said, smiling. Then he ran out the door.